DIABOLIC DOWNLOADS

JIM HALLIGAN

Illustrated by
Fabian Erlinghäuser
The Cartoon Saloon

THE O'BRIEN PRESS
DUBLIN

First published 2008 by The O'Brien Press Ltd,
12 Terenure Road East, Dublin 6, Ireland.
Tel: +353 1 4923333; Fax: +353 1 4922777
E-mail: books@obrien.ie
Website: www.obrien.ie

ISBN: 978-1-84717-065-1

British Library Cataloguing-in-Publication Data
A catalogue record for this title is available from the British Library

1 2 3 4 5 6 7 8 9
08 09 10 11 12

The O'Brien Press
receives assistance from

Layout and design: The O'Brien Press Ltd
Printed in the UK by CPI Bookmarque, Croydon, CR0 4TD

DIABOLIC
DOWNLOADS

JIM HALLIGAN is a teacher and the author of a number of books for children, including *Seeing Red*, and with John Newman: *Fowl Play*, *Round the Bend*, and *Fowl Deeds* (nominated for a Bisto Award). He started making up stories in school to entertain the children in his class and to stop himself from going insane. He's not too sure if he managed to achieve either.

CONTENTS

For Jane, Mark and David and all the stories we tell each other

A pair of glowing red eyes gazed at the world of humans. The babies were restless. They would need young bodies to live in and young minds to take over ... and they would need them soon. The evil red eyes rested their gaze on a town. It was a small town, very ordinary, very normal. It would do ... for a start.

It was time to begin!

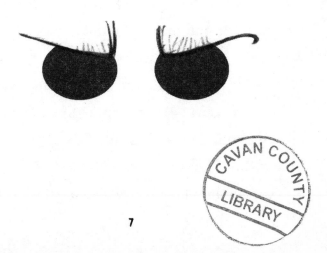

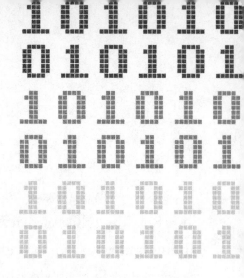

CHPTR # 1

YOU ARE OUT OF CREDIT

Bleepity … blee … blee … bleepity … blee … beep.

In the school yard, a boy froze, dead still, looked around to make sure nobody could see and whipped a mobile phone out of his pocket.

'Yeah! Yes, Mam. Yes, I will. What was that? What? I *still* can't hear you. Speak up .... No. It's this blasted phone! Sorry ... I ... Yes, I *did* close the gate. I swear I did. I'll find Snapper after school and bring him straight home. No ... I won't forget. OK. Bye.'

He quickly switched the phone off and put it back into his pocket. Thank goodness nobody had seen him.

'Hey, Keely! Show us your phone!'

Jack Keely groaned. His phone!

Ross Lacy, Conor Byrne and Judi Carter were smiling at him. Ross and Conor didn't have very nice smiles. He turned away.

'I *said* show me your phone, Keely!' Ross made it sound like an order. Conor grinned. Judi blushed. She didn't like the way Ross Lacy bossed people around.

Jack sighed. Slowly, he pulled the phone from his pocket. Ross and Conor burst out laughing. Judi said nothing.

To tell you the truth it wasn't much of a phone. It wasn't new. It wasn't even second-hand. It was *third*-hand. His two older brothers had owned it before him and they had pretty much wrecked it. The back was held on with sticky tape and the screen had a big crack in it. It only worked sometimes and some of the keys kept sticking.

He had sent a text to his mam the other day …

Yo! in Pat's now when he was going over to a friend's house, but on her phone it came out as … **You Fat cow**. Boy was she mad! Now he had to put up with the likes of Ross Lacy and Conor Byrne laughing at him.

'That's not a phone,' giggled Conor. 'It's a disaster!'

'It's a pile of rubbish,' sneered Ross, 'just like you!'

'Cut it out, you two!' Judi snapped at them. She knew that Ross liked to start fights that he thought he could win. Ross the Boss. He was the biggest in the class and he was always boasting. Judi thought Ross was a bit of a pain. She smiled at Jack.

'I'll bet your phone has lots of great ringtones,' she said to Jack, trying to give him a chance. Bad move! Jack looked down at the ground, wished it would swallow him up and mumbled, 'No, it has just the one ringtone.'

The other two boys hooted with laughter.

'One! Keely, you sap! One! One!'

'Never mind,' Judi cut in with a bright smile. 'You'll be able to get plenty of free downloads from the new phone shop that's just opened in town.'

Suddenly the other two were all ears.

'Free ringtones?'

'Where?'

'How?'

Jack began to breathe again now the two bullies had something else to think about.

'There's a new shop called Nixxter Express just opened on the Main Street,' Judi explained. 'The guy who owns it is giving free ringtones to anybody who calls in and gives him their phone number.'

'I'll bet they're just rubbish old tones,' Ross shrugged, 'just like the one on Keely's crappy phone here.'

'The word is that they're the latest and the best,' said Judi. 'Film tunes, the latest chart hits ... Oh, and you can get free cool screensavers and wallpaper as well.'

Ross and Conor beamed at each other.

'Guess where we're going after school!'

They both grinned as they walked off to tell their friends, their *real* friends, not losers like Jack Keely or that goody-two-shoes Judi Carter.

Judi and Jack watched them go.

'Are you coming down to this new shop?' asked Judy.

'I will if I can find my dumb dog first,' answered Jack. 'He's always running off.'

'I'll help you find him and we can go to Nixxter Express on the way home.'

'Deal.'

'You know, that phone of yours *is* pretty awful,' Judi told Jack.

'I know,' he sighed, and they headed back to class.

***

Nixxter Express was packed. Every kid in town was there and all the grown-ups too; everyone wanted new free ringtones for their phones. There was a huge line of people out the door of the new shop.

Inside, in the middle of the crowd, stood a fat man in a bright yellow and red stripy T-shirt. He had thick glasses and a small beard on the end of his wobbly chin. He held his hands up to the crowd and laughed.

'Take it easy, everybody,' he said, smiling. 'There are plenty of free ringtones for everyone! Just give me your phone numbers and I'll put them into my NEW ... SUPER ... BEST-IN-THE-WORLD ... MEGA COMPUTER and will start download-ing all your favourite tunes and picures to you – for FREE!'

There were two large boxes in the middle of the floor. One had the words 'Special Free Down-loads For Kids' on it, while the other had 'And Free Downloads For The Grown-ups Too' printed on its side in big letters.

Eager hands held out bits of paper with phone numbers scribbled on them. The man took the pieces of paper and popped them straight into the large boxes.

Jack and Judi, and Snapper the dog, had made it into the shop and were waiting their turn. The fat man turned and beamed down at them.

'And what can I do for you? As if I didn't know!' He grinned, and peered at them through the thick lenses of his glasses. Judi handed him her phone number and smiled. Those glasses were odd. For a second, Jack could have sworn that the fat guy's eyes were red. Weird!

Jack frowned for a moment and then pulled his battered old phone out of his pocket.

'Will I be able to get any ringtones for this?' he asked hopefully. Just then Snapper began to growl. It wasn't an 'if-you-touch-my-bone-I-will-be-cross' kind of growl; it was more of a 'I-don't-know-why-
-but-I-don't-trust-you' kind of growl.

The man seemed a bit spooked by Snapper's growling. He quickly looked at Jack's phone and made a face as if he had just been asked to eat a dead rat's guts, but you'd have sworn it was the dog that really upset him.

'That piece of junk?' he sneered. 'Look kid,

I'm a phone salesman, not a miracle worker. And get that stupid dog out of here before I have you arrested. Now, get lost!'

Some people in the crowd laughed. Jack could feel his face going bright red. He put his hand down to Snapper to make him stop growling.

A voice behind Jack piped up.

'Never mind him!' It was Ross Lacy.

The fat man in the bright T-shirt swung around and gave Ross a huge smile.

'Well, who do we have here?' he crooned. His eyes gleamed greedily as he gazed down at Ross. 'Let me see. Yes, that's a nice phone … very nice. For a really *good* phone such as this … I think I'll have to give you *extra special* downloads. Just give me your number. Thank you, young sir. And what is your name?'

'Ross Lacy.'

'Well, Mr Lacy, I'll make sure my computer sends those *special* downloads straight to your phone this very night!' He raised his fat arms over his head and spoke to the crowd. 'Don't worry, especially all you kids! You'll have those downloads coming to your phones tonight ... or my name isn't Nicky Nixxon!'

Then he turned and caught sight of Jack and Snapper, who was still growling like a sports car.

'I told *you* to get lost!' he snapped.

CHPTR#2

YOU HAVE A NEW MESSAGE

Nicky Nixxon was as good as his word. The next day the school yard was buzzing. Come to think of it, the yard was buzzing, beeping, humming, ringing, rocking and rolling. Yep, everybody had their new ringtones, even the teachers. Well ... nearly everybody. Jack winced every time he heard someone's phone going off and playing the latest hit or some cool sound effect. His own wreck of a phone felt like a dead weight in his pocket.

'Wow! Wait till you hear this ...'

'Let's try this one ...'

'Let's swap tones ...'

Oh, it was all too much! He felt sick, angry and jealous – and left out.

Then he heard a voice, 'Hey, there's Keely!' It was Ross Lacy. A group of his classmates walked over to him: Sam, Laura, Darren, Judi and, of course, Ross Lacy and Conor Byrne. Ross was smirking at him.

'What download did you get, Jack?' asked Darren.

Jack sighed. Conor winked at Ross. This was going to be good!

When you're stuck and there's no bluffing your way out, then the best thing is just to face up to it.

Jack gave a shrug.

'To tell you the truth, guys, my phone is an old banger. I didn't get any downloads.'

Judi gave him a wink. Ross and Conor looked a bit disappointed. No fun after all.

'Well, never mind him,' boasted Ross. 'I've got

all the chart hits on my phone. I can …'

Just then, Judi's phone beeped. She pulled it from her pocket and checked. Another download! Ross grabbed the phone from her hand.

'Hey, give it back!' Judi was angry.

Ross pushed her away. 'I want to see what you got.' He began clicking buttons. Judi looked fit to burst. Some of the others backed away. Ross was in one of his moods and that always meant trouble for someone.

'Give Judi her phone back,' Jack said quietly. He sounded calm, but inside he was boiling. Ross the Boss looked a bit surprised, but he gave a quick hard laugh.

'Are you going to make me, Keely?' he sneered. He turned and threw Judi's phone to Conor.

'Hold this for me, Conor. I'm going to …'

Conor's nickname was Butter Fingers Byrne. He was really clumsy. They said he couldn't catch a cold. Judi's phone flew through the air, bounced off Conor's grasping fingers and fell to the hard ground of the schoolyard.

'Now look what you did, Keely!' Ross called over his shoulder as he and Conor ran off laughing.

Jack picked up the broken phone. Judi took it from him and walked off without saying a word.

***

That night, Jack lay in bed awake, wishing he had given Ross Lacy a good thump and wondering did Judi blame him for her smashed phone. Judi lay awake, wishing she had given Ross Lacy a good thump and thinking about the earful she had just got from her mam about that same broken phone. Now it lay in a drawer in her bedroom waiting to be fixed.

Everybody else in the town was sound asleep. Ross was sound asleep. He was a great sleeper. He was pretty good at snoring too. His own super phone lay on top of his locker beside him. It was switched off, but then something strange happened.

His phone turned itself on. The screen didn't go blue, as it usually did. Instead, it was a deep angry red. The phone made a strange hissing, spitting sound … very low, you could barely hear it. It began to rock back and forth, the screen flashing a bright red.

Suddenly there was a POP and a small cloud of red glowing mist puffed out of the phone and drifted to the sleeping, snoring Ross Lacy. It floated over his head for a moment and then just settled on his forehead and sank under his skin.

Ross turned over in his sleep. He gave a little moan and began to snore again, only this time, the snores sounded a lot more like snarls.

Had Jack or Judi looked out of their windows, they would have seen red glowing lights shining in nearly every bedroom window in the town.

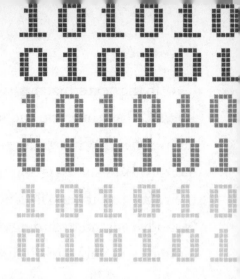

CHPTR#3

DOWNLOAD COMPLETE

Jack was an early riser. He had gobbled down breakfast, fed Snapper (who was whining a lot and seemed upset about something) and headed off to school before his mam or his brothers even got up.

Just around the corner from his house, he saw the first crashed car. It looked as though it had driven straight into a lamp post. Its door was open. There was nobody else about. Jack looked at it for a while, puzzled, and then he moved on.

In the next street there were more crashed cars. It looked like someone had organised a demolition derby. Weird! What was even weirder was the sight of grown-ups standing about with a dazed look on their faces, as if they had no idea who they were. Nobody was complaining. Nobody was talking. Nobody was doing anything. It was as though none of the people knew that there was anybody else there. Come to think of it, they didn't look like they knew *they* were there. This was scary. A hand touched Jack's shoulder ...

'Eeoooowwweeee!' he yelled, nearly jumping out of his skin. He turned, ready to run. It was Judi.

'Take it easy. It's only me,' she said as she glanced nervously over her shoulder.

'Sorry,' breathed Jack, his heart still going like a hammer. 'I thought you were one of those ...' He pointed to the odd, dazed grown-ups.

Judi nodded.

'My mam and dad were like that this morning,' she told him. 'I thought they weren't talking to me because they were still cross about my phone.'

Her phone! He remembered.

'Look, I'm really sorry about the phone.'

'Not your fault, Jack. It was those two jerks, Ross and Conor.' Judi's eyes blazed. 'Wait till I get my hands on them!'

The two walked past the crashed cars and bewildered adults. On the rest of their way to school, they saw even more odd stuff: a bus driven through a shop window; a baker's van stopped in the middle of the road with a trail of buns, cakes and loaves spilled out behind it; a pack of terrified dogs hiding beneath some parked cars and trucks; a postman slowly stuffing all of the letters from his bag into a litter bin. And somebody had knocked down a whole row of streetlamps with a digger. The digger had been left with its engine running in the middle of a traffic roundabout. Round every corner more grown-ups were standing around with empty eyes … all grown-ups, no kids. No kids, except Jack and Judi.

'This is all wrong,' whispered Jack. 'I'm scared!'

'That makes two of us,' said Judi.

They turned the last corner and saw their school. It looked like a bomb had hit it. The whole place was a complete nightmare. Well, come to think of it, it was more like every kid's dream! Windows were smashed; the door looked like it had been flattened by a herd of elephants; lights and signs were dangling off the walls; some of the teachers' cars had been turned upside down. Holy cow! Mr Murphy was still inside his … not that he seemed to mind … not that he looked like he even had a mind! He just stared off into space, upside down, his empty face pressed against the windscreen of his upside-down car as Jack and Judi walked past. Before they could decide whether to help him out or leave him there, they heard a sound. It was coming from inside the school building.

Jack glanced at Judi. She nodded grimly. They were going in!

ROAMING THE NETWORK

The mess and madness outside should have prepared them for what they were going to see next. Yeah, like wearing slippers should prepare you for dropping a brick on your toe. Outside was bad; outside was scary ... but this? This was a whole new ball game.

What was left of the front door had claw and teeth marks all over it. The notice board was in shreds on the floor. There was broken glass everywhere. The lights and light switches were dangling by their wires from the walls and ceilings. Every now and then a loose wire would touch another and start a hissing shower of blue-white sparks. From somewhere deeper inside the building came a droning, humming sound. Jack wanted to hold Judi's hand, but not because she was pretty or anything like that; it just would have made him feel less scared. Instead, he stuck his hands in his pockets, empty except for his old phone.

Halfway down the corridor was a large store-cupboard. One of its doors was hanging open and inside it the two children could see Miss Kelly (third class) and Miss Hannon (fourth class). They looked as though they had just had their cars turned upside down, been pulled out of their cars, then dragged along a school corridor while being pelted with paint, chalk and glue. Yep, that's just about what they looked like. Oh, and they were staring off into space with the same zombie look that all the other grown-ups seemed to have.

'Should we help them out?' Jack wondered.

'They might be better off where they are,' answered Judi.

Further on down the corridor, coat hooks had been yanked out of the walls. Coats had been torn to shreds. Artwork displays lay trampled. Photographs of sports teams and prizewinners, the faces slashed and ripped out, littered the floor. Something awful, some terrible hate had moved down this hallway, destroying everything in its way. The droning, humming sound grew louder.

Now Judi thought that holding Jack's hand would have been a good idea, but not because she thought he was cute, or anything. Instead, she reached out carefully to open a door and ...

Something streaked past them from behind a pile of wrecked coats and pictures. With a demented snarl, Michael Duffy (he was in third class, wasn't he?) burst through the door that Judi had been opening, shoving the two children out of his way as he passed them. Picking themselves up off the floor, they saw him tearing down the next corridor and claw his way into one of the classrooms.

'The little stinker,' said Judi. 'I helped him up in the yard yesterday when he fell. There's manners!'

'No,' whispered Jack. 'He's been changed, like the others we saw outside ... and listen!'

The droning, humming sound was very loud now.

What was it? There was really only one way to find out. They walked slowly down the corridor. The humming grew louder. They reached the door that the boy had gone through. The humming was very loud now. They looked into the classroom.

It was Miss Kelly's classroom, or at least, it had been. Normally neat, tidy and full of bright pictures and things to do, it now looked like someone had stuffed all the bright pictures, toys, games, paints, crayons, chairs, tables and anything else in the room into a small box and then blown it up. There was stuff, or bits of stuff, everywhere. But that wasn't the really interesting bit.

What *was* really interesting was the children inside that room. All of them were from Miss Kelly's third class (including Michael Duffy). Each child was sitting cross-legged on the floor. Each child was facing the same way. Each child was rocking gently back and forth and each child was making that droning, humming sound.

Jack noticed something else.

'Judi,' he hissed. 'Look at their eyes!'

You had to look carefully, very carefully, but if you did, you would notice a dull red glow in the eyes of each one of those kids.

'Jack, this is scary …'

'I've seen eyes like that before,' said Jack. 'Yesterday in the phone shop.'

'Who? One of these guys?'

'No. It was yer man, Nicky Nixxon. Just for a second, I saw it.'

'But what does this all mean?'

'Your guess is as good as mine. Let's see if the rest of the school is like this.'

It was. Classroom after classroom was wrecked

and full of rocking, humming, red-eyed children, many of them still in their pyjamas. In some rooms, one or two children were still battering or bashing or smashing some piece of furniture. A sixth-class girl was swinging from a light in the ceiling like something out of a Tarzan movie. A boy from fourth class had his head stuck down one of the toilets and seemed to be blowing bubbles.

'Ew!'

Then they reached their own classroom. Again, most of their red-eyed classmates were sitting, rocking and humming. There were one or two still moving about. Their old mate, Conor Byrne, was chewing away madly at a table. He seemed to have eaten about half of it, metal bits and all.

Ross Lacy was quite a sight. He was still wearing his pyjamas, nice baby blue ones with a cute dinosaur on the front. He was heading straight for the fish tank where Mr Dunne, their teacher, kept the class pets, three goldfish called Tom, Dick and Harriet.

'Ah, not the fish!' Judy went to stop him.

'Judi! Wait! Don't!' Jack wasn't sure this was a good idea. But as he spoke, Judi had caught Ross by the shoulder of his cuddly baby blue pyjamas and spun him around

Jack was right. She shouldn't have done that. Too late!

CHPTR#5

PROBLEM ON THE NETWORK

Ross stared at Judi for a few seconds. He never said a word; he just stared. He was looking for something. It was as though he was trying to work out just what or who Judi was.

The other children had stopped their rocking and humming. Now they all turned to stare at Judi. Jack took a slow, careful step towards her.

'Judi, move back slowly,' he whispered as Conor dropped the table leg he had been eating.

Not taking her eyes away from Ross, Judi inched towards the door. Jack took her elbow to guide her. All of the other children watched them silently with their dull red eyes. The door was only a few steps away now. They were nearly there. Just a few more steps …

Then Ross screamed. It was the most horrible sound that Jack or Judi had ever heard – a scratching, screeching, scraping noise – like a bus full of seagulls sliding down a cliff. All of the other children got to their feet. The dull glow in their eyes grew brighter. They did not look happy! Ross stopped screaming and then everybody took a slow step towards Jack and Judi. They knew that the two children were different from them. They did not belong; they must be destroyed!

'Jack …'

Judi took another step backwards. Jack stood at the door, still holding her by the elbow.

'Run!' he gasped.

They shot out the door as fast as their feet would carry them, and not a moment too soon.

With a terrible hiss, all of their classmates tumbled out after them. The two children pelted up the corridor. They had walked up it so many times before, but now it seemed like a road with no end. Behind them the hissing grew louder as the children from other classrooms joined in the chase.

As they passed one doorway, some red-eyed children darted out to make a grab at them. Hands clawed at their hair and faces. Jack's jumper ripped as he pulled free only to be caught by yet more clawing hands. Judi pushed hands away from her. Jack gave one sixth-class boy a good thump, but it looked as though he didn't even feel it. He just kept on clawing and grabbing at them. Jack and Judi kept fighting back. It all took only seconds, but felt so much longer. At last they broke free and kept on running.

'Don't look back!' yelled Judi.

'I'm not that stupid!' Jack shouted as they reached the door between the two corridors. Bursting through the doorway, they raced up the next corridor and out into the schoolyard. Seconds later, the mob of hissing, clawing, mad, red-eyed monsters charged out after them. Monsters, that's what they were. You couldn't call them kids anymore.

Right now, they looked like they wanted to tear Jack and Judi apart. There were hundreds of children, but they all seemed to move as though they had one mind – more like army ants than humans.

'They look like they want to kill us,' Judi panted, shocked.

'Well, they'll have to catch us first,' Jack sounded grim. They were nearly at the school gates ...

And then disaster struck.

***

It was only a small rock, lying on the tarmac. Ninety-nine times out of a hundred, Jack would have stepped over it, but not today. His foot came right down on it; he lost his balance, wobbled and fell splat onto the ground. Oooh, that hurt! But this was no time to worry about sore knees. He could hear the snarling mob getting closer behind him. Jack might have lost his balance, but not his wits.

'Judi, RUN!' he bellowed as he tried to pick himself up. The angry mob of red-eyed loonies was only steps away. Judi didn't run. She stopped and dashed back to help her friend.

'Judi.' Jack was too annoyed, frightened and pleased to say any more. He quickly scrambled up, with a helping pull from Judi. They turned to run for the gates and then stopped dead in their tracks.

There was no escaping through those gates now. Their way was blocked and they were cut off. The mob had moved in quickly on all sides. In fact, they were surrounded by a ring of hundreds of hissing, snarling, spitting, clawing demons. Some of the faces in that mad crowd were friends, Laura, Darren, Sam and so many others, but now they all looked the same. Horrible. Determined. No sign of thought, or feeling, or mercy. Judi grabbed Jack's hand. Judy closed her eyes. Jack gulped. The hissing mob had nearly closed in on them. In moments, they would be in arm's reach … and that would be that.

This was it! They were going to die!

***

And then, someone's phone went off. In fact, *everyone's* phone went off, at exactly the same time. The angry, hissing, snarling faces in the mob suddenly looked human for just a split second as everyone reached into trouser, cardigan or pyjama pockets to pull out their phones. Each and every phone flashed a bright red and then the entire mob stood silently, red eyes staring off into space.

Without a second look at Jack or Judi, the whole crowd walked past them and out through the school gates. In moments, the two children were left, alone (apart from Mr Murphy still upside down in his car) in the schoolyard.

'You alright?'

'Never better.'

'What just happened?'

'We nearly got killed by a mob of … I dunno … demons?'

'But we go to school with those guys!'

'Why did they just leave us and go?'

Jack and Judi looked at one another and said the same thing at the same time …

'IT WAS THE PHONES!'

'Of course! My phone is broken and yours is … well …' said Judi.

'It's the downloads.' Jack was certain. 'Now I know where they're all going. C'mon!'

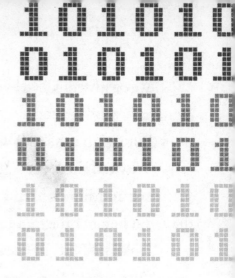

CHPTR#6

THE FINAL DOWNLOAD

They dashed off in the direction of Main Street and Nixxter Express. The town was still very quiet. Too quiet. The only grown-ups to be seen were of the 'I-don't-know-who-I-am' kind. Some were standing, staring off into space, while others seemed to be doing one single task over and over again.

The postman was still standing at the same spot in the street where they had seen him before. His bag was now empty, but he was bending down and putting invisible letters into the same litter bin. A woman was washing a window. Her bucket was nearly empty, but she kept working on the same spot, over and over. The grown-ups were nearly scarier than the demented kids ... nearly.

Just before they turned into Main Street, Judi raised a hand to signal a break. They stopped, panting, at the corner of the street. Both were fairly short of breath.

'Just ... one ... thing,' Judy gasped. 'Why ... *exactly* ... are ... we ... going ... to ... the ... phone ... shop ... again?'

Jack knew what she meant. It didn't seem like the smartest thing on the planet to be heading straight for a mob of snarling loonies who had very nearly tried to tear them apart. In fact, were they out of their minds?

He was worried about his mam too. Everybody in his house might be just as bad as the grown-ups they had seen in the streets. Okay ... so nobody would notice much of a difference with his two big brothers. But what if somebody was hurt, or something, at home? Wouldn't it be easier, wouldn't it be better, wouldn't it be *safer* if they both just ran home and locked their doors behind them? He looked at his friend.

'You think we should head home?'

'I don't know.' Judi had got her breath back now. 'There must be *somebody* we can ask for help.'

Jack jerked a thumb in the direction of a man in a smart suit who was sitting on the ground with one of his shoes in his hands and staring inside it intently.

'Like *him*, for instance?'

Judi sighed. Jack was right. Just running away and going home didn't feel like the right thing to do, no matter how scared she felt. There was no one they could turn to for help. Whatever had to be done to stop Nicky Nixxon, they were the ones who were going to have to do it. She looked at the helpless man, still staring into his shoe.

'I take your point, but what are we going to do?'

'Let's just try to find out what's going on,' said

Jack. He stopped and cocked his head to one side. 'Do you hear something?'

There was a sound, a familiar droning, humming sound, coming from somewhere nearby. It sounded like Jack's hunch was right and all their school friends had gone to the Nixxter Express shop.

'Right,' said Judi, sounding braver than she felt, 'let's go take a look.'

The two children turned the corner into Main Street ... and saw every kid from their school sitting cross-legged on the street outside the phone shop. Just as they had been in their wrecked classrooms, all the children were rocking back and forth and humming. They looked like they were waiting for something to happen. It was a very spooky sight. Jack and Judi crept up to hide behind a parked car and watched.

'Look!' hissed Jack.

The door of Nixxter Express opened and out walked the bulky figure of Nicky Nixxon. The hundreds of swaying children outside the shop became

still and quiet. Not a sound. Not a movement. They all stared intently at Nixxon with their dull, glowing red eyes. He raised his arms and spoke to them in a loud voice.

'Soon, my babies! Soon you will all be free!'

'He's nuts!' whispered Jack.

'No,' said Judi. 'He's up to something. Listen!'

Nicky Nixxon had begun to speak again.

'You are nearly ready for the FINAL DOWNLOAD! When it comes, you will know what to do! Soon you will not need those weak bodies anymore.' Then he began to make the same horrible screeching sound that Ross had made back in the school. It seemed like he was using the screeching to talk to the children. They seemed to understand him. Each child was listening intently to every screech and click that was coming from Nicky Nixxon's mouth. It was like he was giving a speech, but in some very, very strange language.

Jack turned to Judi and whispered, 'Did he say *download*?'

She nodded.

'That means he has to use that big fancy mega computer of his,' she said.

'And we might not be too late to stop whatever he's up to!' Jack rubbed his hands slowly, thinking. 'We have to get into his shop, don't we?'

Judi nodded again. She pointed to a small laneway that ran beside Nixxter Express. There were parked cars all the way to across to it. With luck, they could sneak to that lane without being seen by Nixxon or the other children. Then they could look for a way into the shop. It wasn't much of a plan, but it was all they had. Jack had a thought.

'Eh, are you any good with computers?' he asked, as they crept behind another parked car.

'No,' she admitted, 'but I'm *dead* good with a hammer. C'mon!'

They made it to the laneway and dashed down it. A few steps down the lane they found a door at the side of the Nixxter Express building. Hardly daring to hope that it was unlocked, Jack glanced at Judi and reached for the handle. Back up the laneway, out on the Main Street, they could still hear

Nicky Nixxon giving his screechy scratchy speech. Good. If he was busy yapping away, then he wouldn't notice them sneaking into his shop and finding the mega computer.

The door opened with a quiet 'click'. Great! It swung wide, without making a squeak. Brilliant! Things were going pretty well so far. This was going to be easy! Taking a deep breath, the two children darted inside.

***

Just about then, Nicky Nixxon finished up his speech and turned to go back into his shop.

CHPTR #7

MESSAGE SENDING FAILED

The door to the lane closed behind them and the children found themselves in a small hallway. There were two doors, one to the left and one to the right.

'The one to the right leads into the shop,' whispered Judi. 'I don't remember seeing his computer in there.'

'Okay,' said Jack. 'Let's see where this other door leads.'

He tried the handle and, yet again, the door

opened quietly. In they went. They found themselves in what looked like an office. There was a big desk and a chair. The funny thing was that there was none of the other stuff you'd expect to see in an office: no paper, no files, no pens, no waste-paper bin – nothing. Either Nicky Nixxon was terribly neat or he didn't do much work in here.

It was pretty hard to miss the computer. It stood in the corner on a table on the other side of the desk. It looked cool. It was black. It hummed quietly. It looked like it meant business. It had flashing red lights on the front and it was BIG. When Nixxon had told everybody about his mega computer, he wasn't joking.

'Wow.' Jack was impressed. 'Think of the games you could play on *that*!'

'We're not here to play games!' Judi snapped. Now that they were inside Nixxon's place, she began to feel a bit nervous and worried. The sooner they were out of here the better.

'What? Oh yeah ...' Jack remembered why they were there. He pointed to the screen.

00 : 02 : 57

'Well, his clock is wrong for a start,' he declared. 'It's only about half nine.'

00 : 02 : 53

'That's not a clock,' Judi said, her eyes locked on the screen. 'It's a countdown timer!'

'Oh no!' Jack stared at the screen in horror. 'That means that …'

'Whatever is going to happen,' said Judi.

'Is going to happen in ...'

'Just under three minutes!' she finished.

'Quick! We have to find some way of turning it off!' Jack was frantic. He hated doing things in a rush and, well, if you were going to try and stop some red-eyed nutcase from doing whatever it was he was trying to do, a little bit of *time* would be nice.

Judi looked around the room. There wasn't much to see, just a big heavy desk and a big heavy chair that neither of them could lift. If only there had been a hammer lying around!

00 : 02 : 48

Jack rushed to the keyboard that was sitting beside the countdown screen.

'Let's see if we can shut it down,' he cried, as he began punching madly at the keyboard.

They tried everything they could imagine to turn the mega computer off. They punched every command, every key that they could think of. Their teacher, Mr Dunne, had given them a pretty long list of things you should *never* do to a computer (along with an even longer list of what he'd do if he ever caught them doing it). They tried every single one – nothing. The screen just kept counting down …

00 : 02 : 23

'Drat it!' wailed Jack. 'There must be something we can do to stop this!'

A voice spoke behind them.

'There's nothing you can do!'

Judi and Jack jumped and spun around as though they'd each been stung. In one split, sickening, stomach-turning, horrible, shocking second, they found that they were no longer the only people in that room.

Nicky Nixxon stood at the doorway. His bulky body blocked the only way out, their only escape. They were trapped!

Nixxon smiled. It was the sort of smile that could make you feel sick. He looked so smug!

'You can't stop it now,' he grinned (even worse than the smile). The two children stared at him, silent and scared.

00 : 02 : 14

'You don't even know what you are trying to stop, do you?' he laughed.

'You've done something to all the people in the town,' Judi blurted.

'You've turned all the grown-ups into zombies,' Jack shouted.

'Grown-ups!' laughed Nicky Nixxon. 'I have no use for *them*. They just needed to be kept quiet. It's you kids that I was after.'

'You turned all the kids into demons,' Judi shouted, red in the face. 'You're some kind of devil!'

Nixxon looked at her and snorted.

'Don't be stupid, kid,' he sneered. 'I'm no demon. I come from *space*.'

Just great! They finally get to meet an alien from outer space and it turns out to be a big ugly slob in a horrible T-shirt. Of all the luck!

00 : 02 : 01

'What have you done to our friends?' demanded Jack. 'What do you want with them? And what did you do to everybody's phones?'

Nixxon had sat on the edge of the large desk, still near the door. His eyes grew wide.

'Oooh! Clever kids!' he grinned. 'So you worked

out that I was using phone downloads, did you?'

'But what *for*?' Judi shouted.

'Oh,' Nixxon sighed. 'I might as well tell you. You can't stop me anyway.' He made himself comfortable on the desk. Then he continued.

'My ... people live in space. Most of the time that's where we stay, except for when we have young ones to look after.'

'You've got ... kids?' Judi was stunned.

'Thousands of them!' Nixxon grinned again. 'And right now they are inside all of your little friends out there.' He pointed back towards the street and all the other children.

'You're turning our friends into ... aliens?' Jack was shocked.

'No,' snapped Nicky Nixxon. 'Don't be silly. Our young start off life as tiny sparks of electricity. When I came to your planet a few days ago I found out that you all used electric phones – perfect for storing my babies in!'

'And then you set up this shop and offered everybody free downloads,' said Jack.

'Now you're getting the idea,' Nixxon smiled again.

'And every download was one of your babies?' asked Judi.

'Every download was a *part* of one of my babies. I couldn't fit one in just a single download so I had to send them in a few downloads to each phone.' The alien looked at them with his greedy red eyes. 'But they can't stay in phones forever. They need to grow ... and for that I needed you humans.'

'So the downloads jumped from the phones to the people!' Judi looked disgusted.

'Only to the kids,' Nixxon told them. 'Your human grown-ups are no good for my babies – too slow, too set in their ways to be of any use to me. I needed young, *fresh*, tender, juicy brains that make a perfect home. So it *had* to be kids. I sent mind-blank downloads to the grown-ups to turn off their brains. That keeps them out of my way. I top up the mind-blank downloads every few hours. If not, all the grown-ups would come back to their senses. And we wouldn't want that, now would we?'

OO : O1 : 39

'You said you had thousands of babies,' Jack frowned. 'There are only a few hundred kids in our town.'

'Aha! You humans made it all so easy! Everybody wanted so many ringtones. Everybody was so eager and greedy to swap … and every time they did, I was able to download another part of a baby. As soon as you all went to sleep, my downloads were able to make the jump: mind-blank into the grown-ups' heads and babies into the kids' heads.' Nixxon smiled. 'It seems I missed you two, but it doesn't matter. Some of your little friends out there must have at least a dozen or more of my babies inside their heads right now!'

OO : O1 : 19

Judi glanced at the screen. Nicky Nixxon noticed. She backed away, a little bit away from the mega computer. Jack watched her.

'You want to know what the final download is

for?' he asked. 'Well, I'll tell you if you like,' he giggled. 'It'll help pass the time!'

Nicky was really enjoying himself. Everything was going to plan and these two little humans couldn't stop him. Maybe, afterwards, if he felt like it, he'd eat the two of them. They'd make a nice little snack. Yes! Anyway, time to tell them a bit more about his clever plan.

'The babies aren't ready yet,' he said. 'They need one more download before they can change from being just electric and get real bodies.'

'Where will they get their real bodies from?' asked Jack, but he was afraid he already knew the answer to that.

He was right.

'Oh, they'll start munching and chewing at your little friends out there,' said Nicky Nixxon, as though he was talking about the weather, or something ordinary like that.

'That's awful!' cried Judi. 'You're a monster! You can't do that!' She glanced over at Jack. He gave her a quick short nod. Nicky Nixxon didn't notice.

'Well, sweetie,' said Nicky with a nasty grin, 'I *am* a monster and I *can* do that …' and he glanced at the screen, '… in just a few seconds!'

00 : 00 : 05

00 : 00 : 04

Jack nodded to Judi again.

00 : 00 : 03

Judi took another step back.

00 : 00 : 02

Jack made a dive for Nicky Nixxon.

00 : 00 : 01

Judi swung back her leg …

00 : 00 : 00

… and gave the mega computer an almighty kick just as its lights started to flash and just as it was beginning the final download. Nicky had grabbed

Jack and hadn't seen what Judi was doing. He could see what she'd done now, though ... and he wasn't pleased.

Mind you, Nixxon had *a lot* to be annoyed about. When Judi kicked something, it stayed well and truly kicked. Right now, instead of sending the final command to the alien monster babies, it was doing a really good job of exploding. Little sparks were jumping out the front and smoke shot out the back. It was banjaxed. Not only that, but sparks and smoke were coming out of the light switch and electric socket in the wall of the office. The light bulb in the ceiling popped. Through the window, they could see the same thing happening to street lights. It looked like anything in the town with electricity in it had just blown up.

'Quick! Let's get out of here!' Jack shouted to Judi, but then they both stopped dead in their tracks, staring in horror at what was happening to Nicky Nixxon.

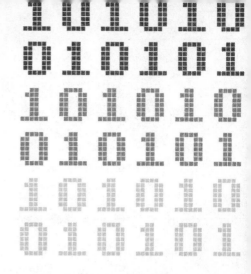

NETWORK BUSY

It's not every day you get to see an alien burst out of its human disguise and change back into its natural (if that is the right word) shape. It was well worth hanging around for. Even so, it's probably just as well that neither Jack nor Judi had had a big breakfast that morning. They watched in horror, not able to move, as …

'Eeewwww!'

Nicky sort of peeled, then poured out of

himself, then swelled up a bit. Then he settled into a big, ugly blob on the floor. Think of a purple-brown walrus with eight arms and a weight problem. Then turn it inside out and give it a pair of red glowing eyes. That's what Nicky Nixxon looked like. And he was hopping mad!

'Look at what you've done! Just look!' he spat. 'My babies!'

'Now look! Mr … or whatever you are.' Jack was red in the face with anger. 'We're sorry if your babies got hurt, but our frie—'

'You dope!' the Nixxon monster cut him off. 'You moron! You sap! They're not *hurt*! Right now, they are all really, really, *really* cross!' The alien looked very, very worried. Okay, so it's hard to tell what a space monster looks like when it's worried. Let's just say that poor Nicky was now terrified.

'I don't get it.' Judi was puzzled.

'Oh, you will!' snapped the alien, wringing all eight of his hands. 'Your little stunt with my computer means that they didn't get their final download.'

'So?' asked Jack.

'So they can't take on proper bodies. So they are running out of power. So they all need to jump back into the phones to recharge themselves …'

'Oh.'

'When *you* broke the computer, it blew up every phone, every light, every TV, every electric thing in the town that was turned on …'

'Oh.'

'Not so much as a light bulb left for them to use for power.'

Jack was beginning to have an idea – something electric?

Nicky Nixxon was waving all eight arms in eight different directions as he shouted, 'The whole thing is a disaster, and I have you two to blame for it!'

'Do you want to go out and see if all your babies are OK?' Judi asked hopefully.

'Are you NUTS?' Nixxon screamed. 'They'd kill me! They need power so badly now they've gone crazy.' He glanced out the window. 'Oh no!

They're starting to jump!'

The children couldn't see it, but hundreds, then thousands, of little glowing red spots of light had started to shoot out of the heads of all the children out on the street. They were zipping about in the air like a swarm of very angry bees.

Jack reached into his pocket. Yes! It was still there!

'What's going to happen?' Judi was frightened now.

'I don't know!' howled Nixxon. 'There's no knowing what they might do. They might all just blow up! Maybe, with luck, they might go hunting for power somewhere else. Oooh, they look cross!'

The swarm of red glowing lights outside was huge now. The children could see the glow through the window, even if they couldn't see the babies themselves. All ten thousand babies had left their human victims and were zipping around in an angry, hungry, buzzing cloud. Their child hosts had fallen like rag dolls onto the ground outside; they were out cold.

'Eh ...' began Jack. 'If it's all the same to you, we might just be thinking of going now.'

'Oh no you don't!' snarled the purple-brown-eight-armed-red-eyed blob standing between them and the door. Judi moved over to stand beside Jack. He gave her a elbow a quick tap with his .... *Get ready.*

'You two aren't going anywhere,' Nixxon went on. 'There's no knowing what that cloud of babies will do and there's no knowing how long they'll stay there.'

'You mean, we'd be safer in here with you?' asked Judi.

The giant purple-brown blob rubbed all eight hands together and said, 'Oh ... I don't think so.' Then Nixxon smiled, showing about two hundred sharp pointy teeth. 'But you two will make a nice little snack for me while I wait for things to die down out there.'

'WHAT?' They were about to be eaten! Jack felt the old worn button on the top of the battered phone in his pocket. He got ready to press it and hoped that the dratted thing would turn itself on, because, if not, what he was going to do next would be really, really stupid.

He took a couple of steps towards the gooey alien ... and all those sharp teeth.

'OK, fair enough, I suppose,' he said, sounding a lot less scared than he really was. 'Why don't you start with me and get it over with?'

'Jack!' Judi was horrified.

'Fine by me.' The monster shrugged, opening his mouth wide, ready to dive on the boy.

It was now or never. Jack pressed down hard on the 'On' button of his old phone. It wasn't much, but right now it was the only thing with a spark of electricity in it for miles around. He hoped it would be enough.

Beeep ... bip beep beep! Yesssss! It had switched on! Jack pulled the phone from his pocket. Nixxon stopped looking hungry and started looking surprised.

'Eh?'

'Here. Catch!' shouted Jack as he threw the

phone into the monster's still-wide open mouth.

Gluummmmp! Nixxon had swallowed the phone!

***

Then lots of stuff happened all at the same time.

For starters, Nicky Nixxon has having a choking fit on the phone. It kept going *Beep bip beep beep* as it rattled around inside him.

The electricity-mad babies outside suddenly stopped their buzzing and zipping. Maybe they could smell the electricity in it, but they were now heading straight for Jack's phone ... and Nicky.

Judi dived over the desk and Jack dived under it. They both made it to the door and bolted out into the hallway, before bursting out into the daylight of the laneway at the side of the shop. Behind them, they could still hear Nicky Nixxon gurgling and spluttering away with the phone inside him.

Just as they got out the door, tiny red sparks began zipping past them. The babies were homing in on their target! The sounds from Nicky changed as he realised what was happening…

'Ghhaak … Splaachht … Oooooooh … Eeeeeeeee!'

Thousands of the tiny red streaks were shooting through the door and into Nicky, all hungry for the power in the phone.

'Time to run?' Jack asked Judi.

'Time to run,' she agreed.

They ran, and none too soon either. Ten thousand power-hungry alien babies must have been quite a squeeze in Jack's poor old phone. It can't have been a whole bag of laughs for Nicky Nixxon either. Anyway …

Kaaabloooooooom!

It was a very big bang. It was enough of a bang to send Judi and Jack flying and to land them in a heap with all the other children.

Jack slowly came to when strong firm grown-up hands helped him to sit up.

'There,' said a kind voice. 'You're going to be fine.'

It was the man who had been staring into his shoe. He was behaving like a proper grown-up. Looking around, he saw lots more grown-ups taking charge and helping other children. Good. At least *they* all seemed to be back to normal.

Judi!

He shot up to his feet and looked around again for his friend.

He saw her sitting on the pavement. She looked a bit dusty, but okay. Judi spotted him and gave him a wink and a thumbs-up. The other children were coming around as well. Nobody seemed too badly hurt, just a bit dazed and surprised. One or two people were sitting, looking puzzled, at the burnt-out remains of their mobile phones. Conor Byrne was howling his head off and rolling on the ground but then, he had just eaten half a table. Some kind ladies were trying to help him to his feet. That was when he saw Ross Lacy.

Some people have nightmares about waking up in a crowded street in their pyjamas, but, for Ross, the nightmare was all too real. He stood there in all his baby blue and cuddly dinosaur glory. Jack smiled. It was going to be very tricky for Ross Lacy to play the hard man after today!

As he walked over to Judi he noticed the firemen standing beside what was left of Nixxter Express. The shop was a mess. Most of the walls had fallen in. One or two loose bricks on the ground were covered in blobs of some kind of purple-brown goo. Out of the corner of his eye, Jack spotted a couple of tiny red sparks on the ground. He bent down to look at them, but, even as he did, they just faded away to nothing.

'I think Nicky and his babies are all gone,' he said to Judi, sitting down beside her.

'Good!' was all she had to say.

'Do you think we should tell anybody what really happened?'

Judi shook her head. 'Who would believe us?' she asked.

'Yeah, you're right,' Jack sighed. The whole nightmare was over. That's what mattered.

***

In a drawer in the locker in Judi's bedroom lay the remains of her phone. She had put it there the day before when Ross and Conor had broken it. It was smashed beyond repair ... and yet, if you listened to it very, very closely, you could still hear, just barely hear, a low hissing, spitting sound. The cracked screen flickered red and then the whole phone rocked slightly.

AN

BOOK!

A BOOK OF MISCHIEF AND MAGIC ...

THE WITCH IN THE WOODS

Marian Broderick

Anna Kelly is a **witch** who's more interested in sleepovers, school friends and soccer than practising her magic. Then she meets Verbena Vile, a **mad**, **bad** and **dangerous** witch – and wishes she'd worked a bit harder on her spells!

When Verbena kidnaps Anna's best friend Mary it's up to Anna and her cat Charlie to rescue her ... with a little help from the **powerful** Mrs Winkle, of course.

Will Anna's **magic** be strong enough to save Mary? Can she and Charlie defeat the vile Verbena?